Salvation

Ryan Parts

Contents

Chapter 1 (Ella)

Ella

I could feel my skin tearing apart from the brutal friction between the rough asphalt and my bare feet. But the pain senses were blocked. My heart was racing furiously inside my chest. How much strain can a heart take? Was I breathing at all? My vision was blurry, but I stared desperately into the impenetrable darkness. My body was trying to tell me to stop. But I couldn't stop. I had to go on. I had to run. To run away.

The leaves of the trees around the road rustled ominously. It was as if they were whispering something to me. It was like someone was whispering from behind.

A feeling of dread had taken over my whole being. A sense of despair and hopelessness raged in my veins. But I couldn't turn back. I couldn't risk wasting even a second. I had to go on. To keep running. To run away.

The moon looked bloody that night. The whole night was bloody. Bathed in the scent of blood. Still fresh on my hands. Fresh still on the snow-white ethereal tulle. On the snow-white long veil. Soaked in the white satin.

It was a bloody night. I was all bloody. But I had to go on. I had to run. To run away.

Black shadows flew high into the sky—the birds of the night. I looked up; it was like they were gathered to celebrate death.

A mighty car horn pierced through the silence, accompanied by the sound of screeching brakes. And light. Right before me. Bright and dazzling. Was that the light of my salvation?

Just a split second. Boom! A little more pain. And then complete darkness again.

***

I opened my eyes slightly. That was not heaven. Was I in hell?

I moved a little. My body responded with a killing pain. I was alive. Why was I alive? Where was I?

My gaze, still not quite able to see clearly, drifted left and right. Dark grey walls surrounded what I could see. Nothing more.

Wait. There was a shadow in front. The shadow moved toward me. I squeezed my eyes and opened them again. It was a man. He stood by the bed I was lying at.

I screamed in fear when I finally managed to focus on the figure. The man was tall. Very tall. Dressed in a black t-shirt and baggy camouflage pants. Dark medium long hair was styled back with a way too large amount of hair detergent. His one eye was covered with an eye patch, and down below, a huge rough scar reached all the way to his chin.

It seemed that he smiled at me.

I screamed once again with a full voice.

"Hello, ma'am," the man said with a husky voice. He really smiled at me.

The stretching of his lips looked so creepy on his face, nothing to do with an emotion that could cause such a grimace.

My voice raised again.

The man sat on the edge of my bed and put his hand on mine. "Shh. Calm down, ma'am. Breath."

"Who are you?" I asked with tears in my eyes. "Where am I?"

"Try not to move much," he said, fully ignoring my question. "You have a broken rib."

Just then, I realized that my wedding dress was gone, and a long nightgown covered my body instead.

"I want to sit," I mumbled while putting the strength to rise in the bed.

"Let me help you." The man offered and reached a hand toward me.

"Don't touch me," I cried out.

"Don't worry, ma'am."

That word ma'am sounded so wrong, given the fact he looked at least ten years or more older than me.

"Tell me who are you!" I insisted, though every word I said came out with great fear.

"I am Cade," the creepy man said. "Do you feel better now when you know?"

I didn't feel any better. I might have been if I was let to hide at the end of the world. "I want to go."

"Why don't you lay down and take a rest, okay?"

The tone of his voice made the words sound more like an order rather than a polite question.

I nodded, and to my brief relief, the man headed to the door.

Just when I saw his back, I swallowed the pain and stood up from the bed.

My life was in danger before. Did the danger grow bigger now? I didn't know how much more pressure I could handle anymore.

The man left the door slightly ajar. Should I try to exit this room? To keep running. To run away.

I took a few steps. Each one caused me an additional ache in the chest. The gray concrete felt cold below my still bare feet. Could I make it exit the room?

The very next move, followed by a sharp, stabbing, excruciating piece of feel gave the potential answer to that.

As I writhed on the floor with drops of sweat all over my face, black leather shoes appeared before my eyes.

Slowly, my gaze slid up over the black jeans, fitting tight on a man's thighs, and stopped on the gun fastened below his leather belt.

Panic aroused, and trembles crept through my whole body again. What a monster I was about to discover next?

Despite the fear, my eyes kept moving above. Hands in the pockets, marked with tattoos, making to wonder if they stopped somewhere or covered the whole area below the shirt colored in black. A metal watch, probably made wholly of gold, embellishing the man's wrist, could have told me what time of day we were in, but instead, I focused on the features. My life lately has taught me to recognize rich people's expensive toys as soon as I see them.

Above the unbuttoned collar, pumped veins stood out all over his neck; I could swear I could see the blood pulsating rapidly in them. A strong jawline defined the bottom part of his face, covered with a black stubble beard. Wet lips, a little slightly apart, damn, for a second, made me wonder how they could taste. But his cold, dark eyes quickly brought back the fear and horror into my heart. A hint of ferocity and cruelty was painted in his gaze. I had already encountered such. From such, I wanted to escape.

How much easier it could have been if that car had killed me that night...

And while this thought was running through my head, I couldn't tear apart my eyes from his.

"Go ahead. Kill me. Just do it quickly. Let's finish this madness," I barely uttered.

He moved back a strand from his raven-black hair that fell over his forehead and extended a hand to help me stand up. Which made things even more tense when I realized I was twice as little as him. Or so it seemed. It was how I felt when my height stopped below his chin.

He reached and moved my face up so my gaze met his again. "Why do you think I want to kill you, love?"

The way he spoke made me tremble again. Were those guys Grayson's men? Only, if they were, I would have been just a memory by now.

"If you don't want to kill me, then let me go. Please, let me go!" I couldn't stop the tears falling down my cheeks.

The man stood still before me, looking intently into my eyes. "You won't go anywhere. At least not for now, love. I have an offer for you."

"What offer? Are you insane? Who are you? Why are you keeping me here?"

"Hear me out," he said calmly. "If you don't like what you hear, you'll be free to go."

I looked down at his gun.

The man grabbed my chin and moved my face back up. "You don't have to be afraid of me."

His words expressed a whole new meaning, far different from the one they were to imply. I was afraid. Afraid of him. Afraid of Cade—the man with the scar. I was scared of the man I was trying to escape from. I was scared of the whole world.

"Who are you?" I asked again. "What could you possibly offer to me? You don't even know me."

"You are wrong here, love." His fingers slid on my cheek, tracing the wet marks. "I know who you are, Ella Zanova. But most importantly, I know what you did."

His words echoed through my head. Over and over again. I couldn't move, I couldn't speak. I couldn't think. I just stood frozen before him.

"The consequences will be very, very cruel. You know that. But, I offer you full protection from Grayson Hall."

"You want to protect me from Grayson? Why?" I asked timidly. "And in return for what?"

"You will stay here with me. Simple as that."

"Why?"

The man pointed with his head to the bed. "There are painkillers on the nightstand. You need some." He reached for the door's handle.

"The offer is valid for twenty-four hours from now. You have plenty of time to think. Until you make your decision, make yourself comfortable here."

Without another word or giving me a chance to speak, he walked out and locked the door behind him.

Chapter 2 (Axton)

Entering my living room, I saw Cade waiting for me, lying down on my black leather sofa with his shoes on top. Damned son of a bitch, he knew how much I hated when he was doing that. "Next time, you will reupholster my sofa with your bare hands."

Cade laughed without making an effort to move even an inch. "Normal people buy new sofas, not reupholster the old ones."

I lit a cigarette and inhaled deeply. With quite good satisfaction, I exhaled after that. "Normal people kill the bastards who don't respect the other's properties. Think about that."

Cade pleasured himself with a big stretch, causing my blood to boil in my veins. Why did this man love so much to get on my nerves?

"Don't freak out, man," he said, finally getting up. "The stress is not healthy. Wrinkles will form on your handsome face."

"Do you have something meaningful to say, or are you about to get out of my house?"

"Let me think about it... Nah, I am excellent here. How did you know it was her?"

"How many women do you think are running around with bloody wedding dresses just right after Grayson was stabbed by his bride?"

"You never told me how did you know that Grayson was injured. There is still nothing on the news."

"I'd got a sixth sense about that," I answered, extinguishing my cigarette in the ashtray.

"Bro, the girl looked terrified. To think I could have run her over with the car... I'm glad she got away with only one broken rib."

"And since when did you have a conscience, Cade?"

"I would never hurt a woman on purpose, Ax! Although she is obviously not so innocent since she'd raised a hand not to someone else but Grayson Hall."

"I don't care about the story behind," I said casually, though I couldn't deny that I was pretty curious about that.

"Why do you want her to stay?"

"If Grayson has let her close to him, to the point that he has been vulnerable, so for some reason, she has been important to him. If that's the case, then I can use her against him one way or another at some point."

Cade went to the bar and poured himself a glass of scotch. "Mhm, typically in your style," he muttered, smelling the golden liquid at the same time. "Let's see how this combination will play out."

I moved to him and took the glass from his hand. "What are you on now, you idiot?"

"I tested the new batch."

I hated his answer and clenched my fists tightly. "I gave you all strip clubs, and you still deal with that garbage?"

"We should keep the streets, Ax! While you play as an honest businessman, new players appear on the street every day." Cade took out a small package from his pocket and reached out to me. "Do you want to try the new formula?"

With a quick swing, I grabbed my gun and pressed it to Cade's temple. "Don't you ever dare to take out these shits in my home again!"

Cade took the package back to his pocket, but not before he reached inside and rubbed the vile substance on his gums afterward. "You are such a killer of the fun, bro." He motioned with a hand to move the gun away from his face.

I looked at my watch—I didn't have more time to deal with him right now. "Go and fuck something to lose some energy, you moron."

"Dahlia is waiting for me at home. She is enough."

"I wonder how the poor girl hasn't broken off her engagement to you yet."

Cade walked down the front door, raising his hand high with his middle finger up. "Fuck you, Axton Dark!"

I chuckled slightly. Going overdramatic was not my thing, unlike Cade's sometimes too-sensitive soul.

More work was awaited for me; the evening was still young. I rushed out of the house.

***

I parked my matte-black McLaren 720S next to the trackage. Only a minute later, the door opened up, and Sebastian came in.

"All clear," he declared.

"Good."

"I am sorry that I had to bring you the news on the phone yesterday, but the tension in the house was mad."

"It's all good. Is Grayson still alive?"

"You know him—he has nine lives, like a cat."

"Tell me about the girl."

"I can't tell you much. I have no idea where she came from. There were rumors that she had been a waitress in a restaurant Grayson used to go to. But I can't tell how accurate this information is. Anyway, one day, a few years ago, she just showed up. Grayson was obsessed with her. What you can think of, he bought it for her. But she... She was... I could tell back then that she was not happy with him. She looked like a good, innocent girl. I didn't know what kept her with him. We talked with the boys, you know, over drinks. Everyone knew she was not a good fit to a mobster. But despite all... No one could predict that she was capable of that..."

"What happened exactly at the wedding, Sebastian?"

"It was right before the ceremony. Someone said that something was going on with the bride. That she was crying in the makeup room. Grayson went there, and we stood in front of the door. He locked, and I guessed he would... he would do whatever he was doing with her. But a few minutes after that, a shout was heard. The voice was not female; it was Grayson's voice. We spent a few minutes until we broke the door, and when we went inside, Grayson was lying on the floor, covered with blood. A knife was thrown beside him. The window was open, and Ella was gone. That was pretty much all I saw."

"Did someone go after her?"

"Numerous men went to chase her, but all in vain. She just disappeared like into nowhere."

"Okay. Thank you, brother."

"No need to thank me, Ax. I owe you my life."

"One thing is to be grateful to someone; quite different is to double-cross Grayson, Sebastian."

"Let me carry alone this responsibility, Ax. Stay safe, brother."

Sebastian went out, and I put my hands over the wheel. My head rested on the back of the seat.

"Stay safe, too, brother," I whispered.

Once, not a long time ago, but long enough to be felt like a lifetime ago, Grayson was also my brother. But what brothers don't ever do, is to fuck off one another.

The engine roar smoothly switched the vibes, and I flew down the highway back home.

Once the camera detected the vehicle number plate, the large iron gates opened, and I parked the car next to my orange Lamborghini.

Opening the vast automatic glass doors followed, leading me directly into the living room. From the couch, which Cade was trying hard to ruin, one could enjoy my proudly owned collection of beasts.

After a few steps inside, my housekeeper, Mrs. Giselle, welcomed me. "Mr. Dark, your guest kindly asked to talk to you."

"Okay. Thank you, Mrs. Giselle."

I went down to the basement floor and unlocked one of the doors.

"How are you feeling?" I asked, looking immediately into the girl's eyes. Why?

"I am not good," she answered. "But that's something I am to be concerned about."

She looked pretty more confident now. Maybe the rest she had taken had brought her some strength.

I studied her features—some strange natural beauty described her face. Not hyaluronic lips, just simple, relatively small ones, yet inviting and juicy somehow. Her skin looked soft, and fuck, it felt soft under my fingers when I got to touch her cheek earlier today.

Her brown eyes also didn't look away from mine, still wet, carrying deep within a tiny spark that seemed to be extinguished a little at a time.

She moved timidly toward me. Very slowly, I knew she was hurt. Her movements caused the silk fabric that fell down her body to outline the perfect shapes she had. A long, messy chestnut hair caressed gently the velvet skin of her bare shoulders.

Despite all that couldn't be denied about her look, she was not at all a typical match neither to Grayson's nor to my taste or to either of our lifestyles.

"Do you really know who Grayson Hall is?" she asked, obviously doubting my words.

"I am the one who asks questions here. You only answer to them. Clear enough?"

She looked down the floor. "How could I know that you can really protect me from him?"

"What do you think am I already doing right now?"

"I accept your offer," she mumbled almost without a voice.

"That's a smart decision, Ella Zanova," I said shortly, trying to suppress the strange urge to touch her face. "Mrs. Giselle will shortly come."

"Okay. May I ask something now?"

"No. But you'll do it anyway. Go ahead, tonight I am in a good mood."

"What is your name?"

"Dark. My name is Axton Dark."

I walked out, not locking this time.

Can't tell I was surprised about the decision she made. No one can save themselves from Grayson alone, let alone a little thing like Ella Zanova.

Chapter 3 (Ella)

Ella

The door opened, and a woman entered the room. Her mahogany hair was styled in an elegant, low bun. Around her green eyes, fine lines gave away that she had probably had about fifty or sixty years behind. The lady looked to be taking excellent care of herself. With a fitted jacket and a knee-length skirt, she walked toward me with a confident step.

"Good evening. I'm sorry if I woke you up." Her voice came out way too gentle and kind than I expected it to be.

And in an instant, it seemed as if the whole room was filled with tenderness and warmth. Or did I start imagining things?

The lady was carrying a tray of food, and the aroma wafting from it instantly activated my primitive sense of starvation.

"I didn't sleep," I replied and waited like a little child for my ration of food.

"Here you are." She handed me the tray and took a few steps back.

Was she about to wait for me to eat, standing right there?

"Don't worry, honey, take your time." She kind of answered my unasked question.

As she walked to the door, I stopped her with insecure words. "Excuse me."

I already knew what I had to do. I had to run away from Grayson, but I had no place to hide. And even if I didn't know who these people were, they were my chance to survive.

"May I speak to..." I didn't even know the tattooed man's name. "...your boss?" That was my guess.

"Your request will be handed on."

I couldn't pay much attention to the way the lady formed her answer because the meal already melted deliciously in my mouth.

After being left alone again, along with the pleasure I gave to my stomach, I couldn't stop thinking if my decision was right. But even if I wanted to keep running alone, I had to heal first.

There were a lot of unknowns; in fact, there were no knowns at all, but as long as I had a roof over my head and obviously water and food, this probably wouldn't work that bad after all. Or at least not deadly, and that alone mattered at that time.

Some hours later, I had no idea how much my savior came.

"How are you feeling?" he asked, once again piercing through me with his dark eyes.

Was there a correct answer to that seemingly simple question?

"I am not good," I answered. "But that's something I am to be concerned about."

No words on his part followed; he just spent an awkwardly long time looking all over me.

I dared myself to stand before him despite how tense I felt when being so close.

"Do you really know who Grayson Hall is?" I asked, just to confirm that I would eventually really be safe.

He looked, however, much irritated hearing about my concerns. "I am the one who asks questions here. You only answer to them. Clear enough?"

His voice came out so rude that it made me regret asking at all. But... How could I know that you can really protect me from him? Without even noticing, that one came also out loud.

"What do you think am I doing right now?"

This conversation was so hard. I decided to quit it already and only to share the decision I made. "I accept your offer," I said, but so quiet that I almost didn't hear myself.

But he obviously heard me clear enough and was not surprised at all, or so he seemed was not.

He complimented the smart decision I made, but I couldn't accept his words as a pure compliment.

When the man was perhaps ready to go out, one more question escaped from my mouth. And since I was allowed to do so, I asked, "What is your name?"

"Dark," he said and paused after that. "Axton Dark."

He gave his answer instead of saying goodbye. At least he didn't lock this time.

The next visitor was not long to come, but this time, I couldn't help but give a little small smile when I saw the kind lady's face.

Her light grace made me feel some kind of calm among this gloomy, dark space.

"How did you like your dinner, honey?" she asked.

"It was very delicious, thank you very much."

She came to my bed. "Come on." Her hand went extended to me. "Let me take you to your room."

"My room?" I asked while slowly standing up. I thought the zone between these four gray walls would be my long-term home.

The lady nodded and gave me support with a hand around my waste.

The long, dark corridors we walked through were as creepy as I imagined the area behind the door would be. But what I didn't expect was what my eyes saw after we went out from the basement.

There was no more concrete; the floor was covered in sculptured marble, so shiny and bright. The surrounding panoramic windows revealed a beautiful night view decorated with hundreds of lights.

The dining area was to one side, and in the middle of the living room was a huge black sofa, in front of which stood a television whose size I couldn't even guess. It was not that I hadn't witnessed such a level of luxury before, but this house was way more stylish than Grayson's was.

Then my eyes stopped at something quite strange—cars were visible behind the opposite glass doors. Why would anyone put their garage as a gallery in their living room?

Well, from what I could see, the vehicles were at least five in number, each worth no less than a six-figure amount, or seven, maybe. Which actually answered my question of why.

Then, my room on the second floor had exactly that fancy style; it was spacious with an incredible interior. I didn't need any convincing before snuggling in the silk sheets' arms.

***

I might have been asleep all night long because when I opened my eyes, there was no darkness anymore. In normal circumstances, I would say it was a beautiful sunny day.

After I rolled over in the soft bed, my body reminded me of my injured rib. But I took another pill, and thankfully, soon, the pain decreased again.

Mrs. Giselle served my breakfast in bed, which was all I could dare to ask.

Just when I was about to swallow my last bit, mighty shouts sounded throughout the whole house. I could already recognize Axton Dark's rude voice.

But I had no guts to show up my face, so I stood in my bed, only wondering what was happening downstairs.

The rest of the day passed no any less different from that when, around the afternoon, I finally gathered the strength to walk out of my room.

Axton was gone, and Mrs. Giselle was also nowhere to be seen. I already had permission to go anywhere around the house, but the basement area was forbidden for me.

Then why my wayward eyes kept looking at the damn door, leading exactly where I shouldn't go?

I tried to distract and explore the interesting living room, which strangeness didn't stop with the garage in it but also at the end, again separated by a glass door, was formed an area with a pole and a jacuzzi in front. My mind imagined a disgusting sight. But it was true how much you can learn about a person just by seeing what their house looks like.

After my tour was over, my legs refused to listen to me anymore, and shortly, I found myself quietly pushing the handle of the door leading to the basement.

"You are dead, Ella. You are so very dead," I muttered to myself while walking between numerous doors.

I didn't dare to open any of them, but a sudden noise drew me to the end of the hall.

There, I didn't have to wonder whether to open the door I was in front of because no one had bothered to close it at all.

My curious mind made me peek inside. Why did my freaking curious mind make me do that?

Axton's massive torso blocked the view at first, but when he moved a little, my heart skipped.

Some guy was roped on a chair and had his hands placed on a counter in front. Blood gushed from one of the wounds on his face, surrounded by many others, smaller ones.

Axton grabbed him by his blouse and shouted something at him; I couldn't tell what because of the shock I was in.

Then, just when Axton moved away, Cade came close only to smash with a hummer the person's hand.

I hid behind the wall and put my hands over my mouth, trying hard to block the scream that wanted to escape.

Not that I could be heard in the background of the man's cry.

My breathing reached the point of its limit, and my heart wanted to jump out of my chest. I couldn't control the shaking of my body.

I started running, making all efforts not to raise any loud sounds until I made it to my room and locked the door behind me.

What did I get myself into? I tried to gather my thoughts. But who was I kidding? I knew very well what I got myself into when I agreed to stay with Axton Dark.

Only, I didn't know why I thought that he could be any different from the monster he was since I saw his true essence the very first time I met his eyes.

Actually, I hadn't hoped that much; at least, the reasonable part of me did not. But the heart was the one to blame that it kept believing that a good side should exist in every man.

Chapter 4 (Axton)

Axton◻

Mrs. Giselle welcomed John Sullivan to my house. Big deals like this one were to be appreciated appropriately with my special aged scotch. For people like John, the time of the day did not matter at all.

I awaited him at the office's opened door, and while we were settling in, Mrs. Giselle had already served a couple of plates of fancy hors d'oeuvres. She withdrew right after that.

The bottle of scotch shone in my hand while I poured John some in a crystal glass. I handed it to him along with the contract and sat across from him behind the massive table.

"Sophisticated as ever," he said while presenting the glass under his nostrils.

"No need to flatter me, John. Let's jump on the business stuff."

He took a small sip and set the glass down on the table. His eye twitched for a moment. That couldn't escape from my vision—my brilliant poker observation could detect even the smallest trembles.

John hesitated for a moment, then moved the papers a bit. I didn't like that at all.

"Listen, Axton. We need to talk."

"No talking, just sign."

"Axton, a change occurred."

My fists slammed on the table surface, and I stood up whole red. "What crap are you talking about?"

John put a finger under his collar to widen the tie knot. "Listen, Axton. Your offer was very high. Someone offered a 30% lower price."

I didn't expect that. That was a sure deal, arranged six months ago.

All of a sudden, my vision went blurry, and my adrenaline shot to its limit. "You, mother fucking bastard! What am I supposed to do with three hundred tons of aluminum now? To put them in your ass?"

"Calm down, Ax, please. We are both businessmen. I am sure you understand."

By the time John finished his sentence, I was already above him. His mouth opened wide with a scream as my hand clamped with full force down on his jaw. My special aged scotch began to fall directly into his throat until every last drop was gone. His face took on a puke-like grimace, but I couldn't care less about that.

"Get out! Get out of my house!"

John pushed the chair in his attempt to get up, wiped his mouth, and stormed out of the office as if being chased by a dog.

I returned to my chair, and Mrs. Giselle brought me my phone without even being asked.

With a voice command, I dialed Cade, and his answer was not long to come. "What's up, bro?"

"I have a little problem, Cade. Someone is trying to screw me up in the aluminum deal. Are you available for some fun?"

"What a question is that?"

"John Sullivan contracted someone else to supply the material. Find out the person's name and have a nice chat with them."

"Got it, Ax. I'll make a few calls and update you as soon as I can."

***

A few hours were needed to have that fucking name. And since the polite conversation between the person and Cade didn't work well, a few more hours later, I got the bastard in my place.

He looked already very familiar with Cade's merciless hands, but still, he didn't want to confess who was behind this.

There was someone behind, that was for sure, since his doubtful "MSSA Global Metal Supply" was created only three months ago.

And offering a lower-than-average market price was not something a new player could afford.

The man welcomed one more fist when he finally decided to talk. "Okay, okay, I'll tell you everything. Just stop!"

Cade took a step back from our guest, who I had comfortably tied up to a chair in one of my basement's rooms.

"Grayson Hall is above. He'll kill me if he knows that I told someone."

Would that son of a bitch ever stop messing with me?

"Okay, listen carefully to what happens now. Your entire batch of material is compromised with impurities and has been rejected. That's what you say to John Sullivan." I grabbed him by his blouse and moved close to his ear. "Did you understand that?"

"I can't do that. I will be dead!"

It seemed that the fool was still more afraid of Grayson than me.

But Cade was good enough to convince him who was worse in this case. His heavy hummer slammed on the person's exposed hand.

"Ahhhh!" A mighty cry came after that.

Cade swung again. "Next one."

"Noo! Don't! I'll notify John about the change! I swear! Just don't do that!"

I blocked Cade's next strike and patted the man on his back. "I knew you'd cooperate."

"Once again, you killed the fun, man," Cade muttered, throwing his hammer on the ground.

"You had enough fun. Now, be that kind to escort our new friend to the exit, please."

***

A good shower made me relax after that. And a few hours of driving completely calmed my nerves.

When the dinner time came, Ella was asked to join me downstairs. Mrs. Giselle presented the meals—a green bean salad for the start. Then, a mix of cheeses and a lobster, broiled to my taste with a glass of fine champagne, could have formed a nice night.

But Ella stood silent and didn't even touch any of the food.

"Why don't you eat, love?"

"I'm not hungry," she answered without even looking at me.

"Do you want anything else?" How more polite could I be?

Her following answer was also short. "I don't."

"How is your rib?"

"What are you planning to do with me?"

More questions again. Already getting on my nerves. She had to learn how to talk in this house. "You don't ever answer my question with a question. Do you understand that?"

"I do."

I had enough of Ella for tonight. "Okay. If you don't plan to eat, go back to your room."

She went upstairs, and I finished my dinner alone. Her gloomy mood made mine the same as hers. I really didn't like the fact that she affected my mind.

Shortly afterward, Cade called to report that everything with the person went well. And since he and Dahlia were in the club, I joined them for a drink.

They were settled in our VIP booth with two more of our most trusted men. Dahlia stood up, and I kissed her on the cheek. "Hello, sunshine, long time no see."

"I couldn't say I missed you at all," she said, sitting back next to her fiance.

"You just broke my heart," I answered, putting a hand over my chest.

Everyone laughed. Before I sat down, I greeted the boys, patting each one on the shoulder.

My drink was already served, and I lit a cigar. "But I sure missed your cocky words."

Dahlia sent me an air kiss. "Always for you, Ax."

"Well, how was the tour, sunshine?"

"Three of the four members of the warm-up band got sick, and we had to do improvised openings for a few days. One concert was canceled because of a storm, and an electric shock burned half my equipment at the last one. All of that aside, the tour was super cool." She shrugged and sipped her cocktail with a straw.

I chuckled slightly. "Sounds like fun."

"You could know that if you had come with me at least once." Dahlia gave us all in a row her reproachful look.

"We also have work, babe," Cade said, burying his face in her hair that fell over her neck.

"I know that, baby. Otherwise, you would be a dead man by now."

"Bro." I turned to Cade. "You have to sleep with one eye open with your crazy lady here."

"Same goes for you, my dearest Ax." Dahlia gave me a wink.

"As we are on work topic, how is your girl doing, bro?" Cade asked.

"Silent and depressed." I shrugged, and I put out my cigar.

"Dahlia, babe, why don't you stop by at Axton's tomorrow to have a chat with the girl?"

"I can do that," she answered Cade but looked questioningly at me.

"Why not? She is about to stay indefinitely anyway. And she might have some information about Grayson that I don't know yet. Perhaps some female conversation will make her more talkative."

"Okay, I'll do that. But here is an idea—why don't you also talk to her?"

"I doubt my way of conducting conversations would make her feel any way better."

"O-or, it's finally time for you to learn how to talk to women in general, for that matter."

"Good idea," I answered Dahlia's remark while I nodded to the blondie who came beside me. "I'm gonna work on that."

I walked toward the club's back room. Kira, the blondie, walked in after me. She was a fabulous chick. With long, slender legs and 400 cc in each breast, blue eyes, wavy blonde hair, and full lips tinted red. Perfect material for every man's wet dreams.

"What can I do for you tonight, Mr. Dark?"

"Get on your knees."

She walked toward me on her fours while I unbuttoned my belt and rested on the comfortable velvet couch.

Her position between my legs was right, and her lips encircled my hard cock; her tongue mastered an excellent play.

I reached over to the side table to pour myself a scotch, lit a cigar, and fully enjoyed the rest of the night.

Chapter 5 (Ella)

Ella▢

Mrs. Giselle came and filled my closet with piles of brand-new clothes. Not that I could show my nose outside of this house, given that hundreds were probably looking for me. But it was good to change the nightgown I was still in.

After taking a shower and making a hard attempt not to think about the scene I witnessed in the basement, I removed my bathrobe and stood before the mirror.

I turned with my back and tilted my head to remember who Grayson Hall was. Some of the marks over my back were still reddish and fresh. Others just reminded me of how long I was trapped in hell.

Grayson had tried to convince me he loved me, and people believed he was in love, but only I knew what was happening behind the closed doors. Each time I didn't agree, no matter the topic about, his belt made me regret that I was alive. And things were getting even worse in the few times I begged him to let me go.

There was no one I could share my pain with because I was alone in this big, cruel world.

Then I breathed a sigh of relief, only knowing that I managed to escape. It took me two years to gather the courage to do what I did, and although my clumsy hands failed to do it exactly right, I didn't regret even for a single drop of blood I spilled out from Grayson Hall.

Now I covered my scars, as always I did, with pieces of clothes to keep them only for me.

When dinner time came, I went downstairs to meet the new monster I was living with.

One evil at a time. At least Axton hadn't raised a hand against me. Yet.

My seat was across from him, on the other side of the long table. Delicious meals were served, but at that time, I couldn't think about eat. Only the presence of Mr. Dark made me sick.

However, what I saw didn't change the fact that I was better here alive, rather than dead outside. So, I stood quietly, hoping the time would pass quickly.

But at some point, Axton broke the silence. "Why don't you eat, love?"

"I'm not hungry," I answered without even looking at him.

"Do you want anything else?"

Why did he bother to ask? "I don't."

"How is your rib?"

My rib would heal. But what after that? He never really shared why he offered his help. Someone like him can hardly do something without benefits. "What are you planning to do with me?"

His anger came in return. "You don't ever answer my question with a question. Do you understand that?"

Good job, Ella! Keep challenging him, and he'll bring you back to the basement to meet the fate of the unknown man...

"I do," I confirmed with a shaking voice.

His following words made me relief. "Okay. If you don't plan to eat, go back to your room."

I did exactly that. I went to my room, waiting for one more night to go.

***

A knock on the door marked the start of the following day."May I come in?" a beautiful girl asked, staying by the threshold.

It wasn't hard to recognize the famous singer whose songs were my best friends during the past years. But what was Dahlia Lee doing in my room?

She looked exactly like in her video clips, but somehow, even more mesmerizing in person. Her eyes shone in variegated blue-green tones, highlighted with light and delicate make-up. Every other part of her face was also like drawn by a painter—from her perfect-shaped brows to her full pink lips.

Her modern fashion taste was evident by the combination of short brown leather pants and a white cropped top over which she wore a leather jacket with one fallen shoulder. High heels further accentuated her slim and perfect legs. Although her ginger hair was tied up in a high ponytail, it was visibly apparent that it was stylized with great care.

All of the above made me realize how plain I looked compared to her. I have never had a reason to think of what I looked like; that's why I never understood why Grayson wanted me at all.

But that did not matter anymore. The question now was why Dahlia Lee stood in front of me.

"Of course, you can come in." The words were finally uttered from my lips.

"Ella, right?" she asked while closing the door.

"That's me."

"I am Dahlia." She presented herself, which I already knew, but her next addition left me quite shocked. "I am Cade's fiancée."

"You are Cade's fiancée?" By the time I asked in surprise, I remembered Axton's words. "I am sorry. I forgot I am not supposed to ask questions here."

Dahlia sat on the armchair opposite mine. "Axton's requirements?"

I shrugged. "His house, he determines the rules."

She slapped her forehead. "Why am I not surprised?"

Was I supposed to respond to that?

"Anyway. Yeah, Cade and I are engaged." She added right after that.

That sounded strange. I couldn't imagine them side by side. They looked so different, as different were the day and the night. But that was a personal choice, if that choice, of course, has been made by her will. Considering what I experienced, it wasn't hard to believe that there were more girls like me.

But the way she said they were engaged, however, came joyful and happy from her mouth. So, perhaps it was really a personal choice, and that was not my business at all.

Going back to my concerns. "I am sorry, but I don't understand why are you here. Do you want something from me?"

"Cade asked me to come. He was worried about you."

I got ashamed of my subsequent reaction when a loud laugh split out from my mouth. Cade was worried about me? Cade with the hammer, the same Cade?

"I am sorry." I tried to apologize. "It was not on purpose. It's just... Cade and Axton don't look like people who worry about the others."

"Why do you think like that?"

Why?

Was this girl falling from another planet? Even I, who met them a few days ago, knew what type of people they were.

But I kept my answer to myself; I had no right to talk to a stranger girl against her man.

"They are not that bad, as they look." Dahlia continued the conversation. "Give them a chance. But in the meantime, if you need something or someone to talk to, you can ask Mrs. Giselle to call me anytime. I will come as soon as I can."

That sounded kind of her, although I still couldn't understand why she would do that for me.

"Thank you," I replied anyway.

"I gotta go. See you soon, Ella."

"Dahlia, wait. Do you know what exactly Cade and Axton do?"

Her expression drastically changed. "I don't mess with my fiancé's business just like he doesn't do it with mine." She forced herself to smile after that. "Have a nice day, Ella."

"You too," I said in response.

Dahlia left, and I felt regret that I maybe offended her with my reaction about Cade. I could have asked her about her career instead, to get her sign or even to ask her to sing. But my stupid self decided to doubt every word and every action of those whom I met.

The hours flew by while I stood alone in the room, thinking and rethinking about what I should do next. But no answer did come.

I took my daily walk around the house and the backyard. Then I walked into the garage and slid a hand over the tops of the luxury vehicles. How much money was spent there to make someone happy, while to many people, happiness consisted only of having someone...

"What did he do to you?" Axton's voice interrupted my thoughts.

"What do you mean?" Wrong again, Ella. Question again...

But no remark followed. "Did Grayson do something to you, or did you go to him with a premeditated plan to kill him? I can bet it was not the second guess."

"Grayson is a bad person, and he deserved what I did," I answered, and the tears in my eyes began to grow again.

"The world is full of bad people, love."

I looked Axton in the eye. "Only bad people I know."

"I told you not to be afraid of me."

"You are not any different from Grayson." The words split out of my mouth. "I saw you. I saw what you and Cade did to that man in the basement."

I hadn't finished my sentence when, with a sharp move, Axton pressed me against the wall, encircling my throat with his hand.

"How dared you go there?"

I squeezed my eyes, ready to welcome the pain.

He kept shouting. "I told you you are not allowed to go in the basement!"

His voice was terrifying, reaching tones that could freeze the blood. I still felt the pressure of his touch on my skin. But I didn't feel any pain.

My eyes opened timidly, slightly, still very moist, to stare into his black, dilated pupils. I couldn't explain what level of rage his gaze was broadcasting, but his hand did not hurt me at all.

Chapter 6 (Axton)

"Thank you for accepting me, Axton." John Sullivan stood in the doorway. "I'm sorry to come without an appointment."

I expected his visit anyway. "For you, I am Mr. Dark."

"Mr. Dark... Okay." John stepped uncertainly into the room. "I understand you are upset. But I made a mistake, Axton." He cleared his throat. "I meant Mr. Dark. I shouldn't have trusted people I don't know. Damned to be my greed. They canceled the deal due to problems with the material."

Really? What a surprise...

I walked to the counter and poured myself a drink. "So, what do you want from me?"

"Let's renew our work together. You would never make a compromise with the quality of your production."

"Hm..." I sipped without giving a response. Watching John sweating gave a great pleasure to my eyes.

"Listen, Mr. Dark. I have to deliver the material. My clients are not exactly patient people. I know you'll understand and forgive my mistake."

"Alright. Alright. Calm down, Sullivan. I understand. Everyone makes mistakes."

John breathed a sigh of relief while I opened the cabinet and took the contract out of it.

"Phew." The sound came loud as he wiped his forehead. "You are a decent person, Mr. Dark. I knew you wouldn't let emotions get in the way of the deal."

"Sure." I presented the contract, opened on the last page, along with a pen. "But a change occurred."

John stopped right before he placed his signature. "What do you mean?"

"The price jumped double high." I opened the first page and pointed to the paragraph.

"What? Even my percent can't cover the difference."

"I know. But you also have to know something about me, John. People, who screw me up, I screw them up twice. Now, sign or go—it's your choice."

The outcome was clear. He was trapped in a dead end. There was no time to look for another manufacturer, even less to wait for the time needed for pre-production arrangements. Well, he surely could cancel his clients' order, but I guessed he loved his head more than the money he just lost the chance to gain.

And although I started to get annoyed watching his trembling hand, I waited politely for him to put his sign next to mine on the page.

"Smart decision, John. It was a pleasure to do business with you."

Sullivan walked out of my house, still silent, with a head down. I sat on the chair and leaned back, looking at the glass in my hand. Yeah, deals like this one deserved to be appreciated with my special aged scotch.

That was an excellent start to my day.

People had to know they couldn't mess with me. John Sullivan and those who would come after him. I kept my word, and I hated it when someone did not. Now, the lesson was taught.

As I walked out of the room, Dahlia suddenly blocked my way. I'd forgotten she would come today.

"Good morning, sunshine."

"Don't 'sunshine' me, idiot. I met the girl. She is scared of both of you. What did you do? Will you ever start to behave?"

I walked past her, not paying attention to her words. Dahlia's melodramatics. She and Cade were a perfect match.

"Don't walk away, Ax!" She caught up with me. "Make an effort and talk to her. She is your guest."

"She is not my guest. She is..." I couldn't exactly come up with a term for what Ella Zanova really was.

"Please. Can you imagine what she is going through?"

"Everyone is going through something, sunshine."

"Don't give me that crap! You're going to talk to her."

There was no point in arguing with Dahlia; she was already on a mission to save the world.

I admired her passion and her pure soul, which remained uncorrupted over more than two decades.

We met when I was ten—four years older than her. She was a sister to my best then-friend. Actually, he stood as such till his very last breath. I was not sure if he would think the same for me if he'd made it alive, but God is a witness that I would save him if only I could.

We were three brothers then, and in an instant, only I left. One went dead, and one deserved to be dead instead. But life was not fair. I never doubted that.

Dahlia suffered most then—she lost pretty much everyone she cared about and was stuck only with me. Well, Cade fit right into the plot, and the two have been in love ever since then. She deserved someone exactly like him, or at least who he was before he came back from the war.

But that made him my right-hand man. We had known each other forever, and I've always considered him like my brother as well, but he was never involved in my world till the moment he realized that he belonged exactly there.

Dahlia shone over the years like sunshine in our dark world to keep the last drops of humanity we had left. At least, she believed that there was such a thing somewhere inside us.

"Okay. I'm gonna talk to her. Be calm and go to annoy your man."

She sent her typical air kiss and went on her way.

***

There were more tasks I should have dealt with during the day. The aluminum factory was not my only thing. In fact, it was the smallest business of mine. I've been working hard over the last few years to make everything legal. Arms production was one of my most significant personal achievements.

My father bequeathed me a lot. Everything I had, I had it from him. Everything I had learned, I had learned it from him. But since he was gone, I managed things my way. Well, there was always someone to challenge me, and I had to respond accordingly, like in the Sullivan case. But that was my nature, which was something I didn't try to change. One thing was to do business honestly; quite different was to get soft.

After Cade and I tested the new arms, the long day came to an end. When in the evening I finally parked in the garage, Ella was there. She didn't even hear me; she looked deeply immersed in her thoughts.

I went a few steps close—a silent sadness radiated from her. Was Dahlia right—was there still a humanity part in me? The feeling I felt when I saw her was strange. I haven't felt that way since... since actually never.

"What did he do to you?" I asked.

Ella turned her face and looked directly into my eyes. "What do you mean?" Right after that, she lowered her gaze.

"Did Grayson do something to you, or did you go to him with a premeditated plan to kill him?" Looking at her innocent expression, it was hard to think that she could make a plan to kill someone. "I can bet it was not the second guess."

"Grayson is a bad person, and he deserved what I did."

Ella was right. Grayson deserved that. He deserved to suffer, to be drowned in his blood without a drop of mercy till the last bit of his breath left his lungs.

But she didn't seem to feel exactly my way. Tears glistened in her eyes.

"The world is full of bad people, love."

Once again, she looked at me. "Only bad people I know." Her words sounded experienced, suffered; they sounded insurmountable, being said with a quiet voice that seemed to want to be screamed.

"I told you not to be afraid of me."

"You are not any different from Grayson. I saw you. I saw what you and Cade did to that man in the basement."

By the end of her sentence, my blood started to boil, and everything turned black. Without trying to think, I pressed her against the wall and put my hand over her throat. "How dare you go there? I told you you are not allowed to go in the basement!"

But her shaking body under my hand made me realize how much she was really afraid. Eyes closed, squeezed, like in anticipating... for a hit?

Not obeying my rules was something absolutely forbidden that resulted in losing my temper, but for fuck sake, I knew how to deal with it. Only a few have dared to do that, and to their great regret, it was the last thing they did. But I have never ever been in a situation this to come from a woman. I was not sure how to handle this now, but what I wouldn't do was hurt her somehow.

That's why I never allowed a woman close to me. Women are for pleasure and only for that. No chance for dramas or any shits. Because, when shits happen, a fucking man I would hit, but fucking woman I could just not. Fucking Ella Zanova...

She opened her eyes timidly. They were still wet. She locked them with mine, but there was something different in her gaze. She was surprised—maybe she really expected things to get worse.

I stood still for a few more seconds, looking at her. Then I loosened my grip and slowly moved my hand away from her throat. "Get the hell out of here! Go back to your room. And don't you ever dare to do something I haven't allowed!"

Chapter 7 (Ella)

Ella

Axton ordered me to go to my room. So, I did.

I closed the door of my room and leaned against it. But for some unimaginable reason, my body did not shake. My heart rate stood calm inside my veins. Only my stupid heart was whispering annoyingly in my chest. You did wrong, Ella. You did wrong. You had to apologize.

When I walked out of the room only a very few minutes after going inside, another thought crept through my head. That's what exactly the masochists do—after they narrowly missed it once, they go to look for another trouble right after that...

But he didn't hurt me. The scene kept repeating in my head. He did not. And that made the difference for me.

This didn't make Axton any good person, or hell did not make what I saw right, but damn it, he made me feel bad that I went against his will.

I had to apologize. Stupidly, as stupid I was. But I had to do that.

When I went downstairs, Axton was no longer in the garage, nor could I find him anywhere around.

Just when I was about to return upstairs again, Mrs. Giselle went out of the kitchen. "Hello, honey. Do you need anything?"

"No. I mean... Yes. I was looking for Axton. Um, Mr. Dark. Do you know where he is?"

"He went to the lake. Perhaps he is swimming with Amara."

Amara? Who was Amara?

"Okay. Thank you, Mrs. Giselle."

The lady followed her way while I stood for a while in hesitation. Anyway, whoever Amara was, I shouldn't go to them, that was for sure.

But... I went.

The bright yard's lamps enlightened the beautiful gardens around the alley. Unique exotic flowers made the environment feel like I was in paradise. The babbling of the small stream echoed softly from the distance.

I walked lightly and quietly, very timidly, towards the end of the yard, where a vast artificial lake was built. It was different there, quite dark and gloomy, even frightening, I could tell. The light was minimal and dimmed, only to see where exactly you stepped. Only the current full moon reflected on the water's surface.

I'd been there once, but even during the day, the area gave me chills. It looked wild with tall vegetation, in total contrast with the perfectly manicured and mowed gardens a few meters away.

A big tree provided a cover for a while while I tried to see if there was anyone in the lake. But the water seemed calm, no movement or sound.

Not long after, Axton appeared, swimming alone. I breathed a sigh of relief. What was that for? No Amara, okay. But he for sure looked like he could have dozens of women and even at once, which probably he did. I didn't like where my thoughts were going at all. Perhaps there was a reason behind that, a lusty reason, so unreasonable somehow. But damn it, even in that darkness, some lights crept through the space to illuminate his strong arms and muscular chest. And that perfectly tanned skin, so wet, covered with drops that glistened discretely with each and every move. But then, each of these moves screamed predator, and that's what he was. So, why did my eyes refuse to look away from this devilish man?

"What the hell are you doing there?"

I jumped in surprise. I was hidden, wasn't I?

"I..." With uncertain steps, I walked out from the shadows. "I was looking for you."

"Wasn't I clear enough?"

"Yes. But I... I wanted to apologize." I tried to sound as confident as I could, but everything came out in a whispering tone.

"You wanted what?"

Did he not hear me, or just wanted to make me repeat that? "I—"

I wasn't able to finish my sentence because, as if from nowhere, two eerily eyes shone behind Axton. "Ahhhhhhh! Ahhhhh!" I managed to give a little pause through the panic I felt, only to catch a bit of breath. "Ahhhhhhh! Get out of the water! There is... Ahhhh!"

"Did you lose your mind?" Axton asked and reached toward the creature, which was already right beside him and stroked gently its head. "You'll scare Amara."

"This..." I took a few steps backward. "This is an alligator!"

I rubbed my eyes and shook my head a couple of times. Did I see right? "Oh, my God! You are touching it! Why do you do that?"

"For fuck sake! Shut up! She has to be afraid of your fucking screaming, not you to be afraid of her!"

Axton patted the alligator, and it swam down till it merged with the darkness. Then he got out of the water and once again walked toward me, full of rage.

But at that moment, I was more afraid of Amara, which would have been way better if was simply a woman, not a reptile. "That was... That was a real, alive alligator..."

Axton reached his hand but squeezed his fist just before he touched my skin. His eyes shut closed.

"I..." I continued to mumble. "I walked here the other day. Why did no one tell me that I could be torn apart from your... what is it, your pet?"

"Did she do something to you?"

"No."

"So what those screams are about? She hides when someone comes close, so there is nothing to worry about."

"Nothing to worry about? These animals are cold-blooded killing machines that are not able to be domesticated."

"Not this one. Don't come here if you are afraid. End of conversation."

I narrowed my eyes. This man was a complete psychopath.

But he hardly cared about what I thought. He turned his back and started down the house.

"Oh, my God, Axton! Don't leave me here!" I ran after him and clung to his hand.

Of course, I did expect some rudeness in response, but we kept walking that way until we went inside. Finally, in a safer place!

***

The following days passed by. They turned into weeks. Weeks turned to more than a month.

I hadn't spotted Axton many times, which was actually based on the fact that I had left my room only a couple of times. Only the thought of Amara could make my heart stop with fear.

Mrs. Giselle was kind enough to bring me meals upstairs. She and I used to exchange a few words every now and then, not something specific, just casual themes. A doctor came twice to check up on me, bringing me the news that my rib was completely healed.

Although I spent that time stuck in the room, only watching TV or reading a book, and regardless of the gator outside, I felt way more free than I ever have felt in my life. Stange irony, wasn't it?

There was no one to tell me what to do. There was no one to force me to do what I didn't want to.

Still, some nightmares were worse than others—when Grayson was finding me and tortured me to death, then bringing me to life, only to repeat the process over and over again. But in all the following mornings, everything was just bad dreams and nothing more.

Once, I asked Mrs. Giselle to call Dahlia, and she came the next day as she'd promised to do. Then she kept coming for many more days after that.

Talking to her was nice and refreshing, and her stories made me imagine the world in a light I never knew about. She showed me photos from her concerts and adventures, photos with fans, and such of video clips filming processes. It looked exciting and much of a fun, even the failures and the hard times. Everything was a part of her own journey, her dream, and her way to make it true. Two words made possible that—own will—that was my dream.

Dahlia was also afraid of Amara; she admitted today when I asked her about it. But she made efforts to assure me that what Axton told me was truth. The alligator has been there since it was a baby and has grown up under the care and love of its owner.

Axton and love? Okay. If Dahlia said so…

"How long do you know Axton?" I asked her.

"From a very, very long time." She didn't need much conviction to open up before me. "We grew up together. Axton's father took my brother and me under his wing, along with... along with another guy, and we all lived like one big happy family."

"Another guy? You mean Cade?"

"No. Cade was Axton's friend, but he was not part of... of our family, let me put it that way. I have seen him a couple of times throughout the years, but he didn't come often into the house."

I crossed my legs under each other on the bed and asked curiously, "So, how did you two get together?"

"Eight years ago, Axton's father passed away. Almost right after that, some terrible things happened that changed our lives completely. My brother died. Amelia, Axton's sister... she..." Dahlia's eyes filled with tears.

"I am so sorry for your loss."

"Thank you. It's hard to go back to that time. Anyway. I was devastated. One day, Cade came to the house, and the rest is history now."

The tears disappeared the moment she said Cade. That sounded romantic, I couldn't deny it.

"He was the nicest person I knew. Like an angel. He looked like one. With the most beautiful face. He could have made a great career in modeling for sure."

"What happened to him?"

"Well. Unfortunately, he was not a model; he was a soldier. When he was assigned to participate in the war in Afghanistan, he did not hesitate whether to accept to join the mission or not. He went and spent a year there, seven months of which in captivity.

"They saved him at last. And they brought him back to me. In pieces. Disfigured. Half-man, half-corpse."

I listened in silence, and Dahlia's pain pierced me deeply.

"Axton hired the best plastic surgeons from around the world who performed dozens of surgeries to make Cade look the way he does today."

I felt so bad about the way I reacted the first time I met him. "I had no idea."

"You couldn't have known. But I don't care about his look. My love for him hadn't changed. He had changed, yeah, but our love had not. We suffered a lot while he was recovering. But I was happy and grateful to have him back. Alive. That's all I care about, Ella. To have him alive by my side."

"Dahlia, I am so sorry."

"Don't be. Everything is perfectly fine. Now,"—she wiped her eyes and reached to take her bag—"I almost forgot what I came for. We are going out tonight, a-and you are coming with us."

"Um... Dahlia... I can't. I mean, I can't go out. I don't know what Axton told you... I don't even know what exactly he knows, but there are people who are looking for me."

"I am aware of that. That's why—ta-da!" She took out something from her bag and threw it to me.

"What's that?"

"Open it!"

I took out a black colored wig. Dahlia didn't wait and grabbed my hand, causing me to stand up. We stood before the mirror, and she tied my hair and put the wig on my head. I couldn't believe how transformed I was only with this bit of change. My hair was quite shorter now, barely reaching my shoulders, so dark and straight. Thick bangs almost covered my eyebrows.

Dahlia placed a container of colored contact lenses on the dressing table in front and put black sunglasses on my eyes. "A little bit of makeup and no one in the world could recognize you. What do you think?"

My lips stretched into a wide smile. So wide that it felt like the corners of it were touching my ears. "It's amazing! Thank you, Dahlia! I can't believe I'm going to be able to go outside!" I turned to her. "Does Axton know about this?"

"Ahem." She bit her bottom lip. "Ma-a-y be..."

"What does maybe mean?"

"Well. He doesn't know. But he'll learn any moment now."

Chapter 8 (Axton)

Axton

After a month, I sent the production on the docks and took a quiet perverse satisfaction after sending a quiet message to Grayson to fuck himself.

Usually, I didn't regret any action of my life, but I'd never forgive myself that I didn't kill that bastard the night when I had the chance.

This was what happens when you go soft. When you don't want to believe that the one you considered your brother betrays you in the most unceremonious way. The one you fought side by side with, the one you were ready to die for.

It was a single moment of weakness that has unfortunately haunted me ever since.

But sooner or later, his time would come.

As the ships moved away, I also moved away from the docks. I revved the engine a few times and drove off on dirty gas.

As soon as I returned to my house, I noticed Dahlia's car on the central allay. My hands gripped the steering wheel tightly as I passed her Mercedes and precisely parked my car on its spot in the garage.

I couldn't tell if she was doing it on purpose. Was driving a few more meters down and parking in the parking lot that hard?

"Dahlia!" I shouted the moment I entered the living room. "Get your fucking car out of my alley, or you'll find it in pieces next time!" Since she was not there, I shouted once more, "Dahlia!"

A few seconds later, Dahlia showed up from the second floor. "Calm down, jackass! They heard you even on the other end of the world."

Her way of addressing me did not affect me at all. Since we were kids, she and my sister used to call me with nice names every time I'd yell at them. Sometimes, I even received a blow or two in the chest, but their tiny fists only managed to cause me a tickle.

Once, the two united and attacked me like lionesses from both sides.

Of course, it didn't take much effort for me to lift each one in the air

and throw them into the pool. But the damn girls managed to drag

me down with them. I chuckled a little; those were good times.

"The car, Dahlia!" I went back to the current situation. "I'll use Cade's

hammer to smash it next time."

Dahlia took a few steps down. "I liked the newest Bentley, so go

ahead. This pleasure of yours won't cost you more than three hun-

dred and fifty K bucks."

"I'll buy it for you, and then I'll smash it too."

"You are such a twisted person, Ax. You know that?"

"Thanks. Now give me the key to move the fucking car."

"Screw the car. I want you to see something." Dahlia stood beside me

and placed her arm over my shoulder. "Ella!"

"Damn it, Dahlia! Don't scream like that!"

"Ha! Way to feel how I do when you shout."

"I doubt my voice is that annoyingly shrill."

"Nope. You are naturally gifted to sound like a monster, even when you talk. But look up now."

My gaze moved to the direction Dahlia pointed with her head. Ella stood there on the highest step of the stairs.

There was no mention of her simple vision anymore. A short black dress was clingy over her body. A deep V-neckline accentuated her small and firm breasts. No bra underneath; her nipples were delicately outlined below. Her feet stepped on high, thin heels, and fuck, for a moment, I imagined them pointing up.

There was makeup on her face, I noticed when she approached me. Not too much, just enough to highlight her natural features. Her eyes were different, a green color now, but her gaze still radiated thrills. Much shorter than it had been before, her hair contrasted in black.

"So, what do you think?" Dahlia asked.

I skipped her question and addressed Ella instead. "Why do you look like that?"

"I—" Ella tried to speak, but Dahlia interrupted by hitting my arm with the back of her hand.

"He meant you look beautiful, Ella."

Fuck, I meant she looked very damn hot, and for fuck sake, she was now even more beautiful than she had been before. "I meant what I meant. Now explain why is that for."

"I invited Ella to join us tonight. That's what this is for." Dahlia answered. "And I don't think someone could recognize her, plus she'll be safe with us."

"Do I look like a fucking bodyguard?"

Dahlia stood before me and squeezed my biceps. "Yeah. I think you fit into that."

Ella took a few steps back. "I am sorry. I shouldn't agree. This is a mistake. I shouldn't come."

"Yes, you should, and you will." Dahlia turned to Ella. "Axton meant that if someone dared to reach out to you, he'd beat them up." She then looked back at me. "Right, Ax?"

Fuck you, Cade, that you proposed your thing to come here and mess with my stuff!

"Someday, I swear, sunshine, you and your beloved one will disappear from my life!"

"Then there will be nothing to live for, so be careful what you wish for, Ax." Dahlia kissed me on the cheek. "Nine o'clock in the club. Bye-bye now! I am going to move my fucking car."

Dahlia walked out, and I wondered whether to laugh or shout after her.

"I still think it would be better if I don't come," Ella said, shifting her legs. She didn't look comfortable at all.

"If Dahlia wants you to come, you can come if you want. She did a good job and is right that it's hard for you to be recognized."

That sounded strange coming from my mouth. But as strange as it was, it was stupid as well. Ella shouldn't go out. Along with the fact that Grayson was looking for her, she was a trouble for me since day one.

"Actually, I really want to go out. Thank you for allowing me to do that. I am just gonna change that dress." She looked down.

"Don't. You look good. You don't have to be ashamed of that."

"I..."

"The car will be waiting for us in an hour."

I went to my room and took a cold shower. I didn't like how much I liked how she looked.

***

Twenty minutes before nine, there was a knock on my door. I opened it while putting on my shirt at the same time.

"I am sorry to bother you, Axton." Ella stood outside, talking uncertainly as always she did. "I didn't know where to wait for you, and I am afraid to walk in the yard alone."

"Amara can't come either in the garage or out front of the house."

She looked down again. Fucking Ella Zanova! Did I already say that? Why's this fucking urge to make her feel safe.

I took her chin and moved her head up. "Anyway. I am ready. Let's go."

We got into the car, and before long, we were at the club. Dahlia and Cade were already there.

We exchanged the usual greetings, and Cade reached out to Ella to take her hand and kissed it after that. "Good evening... Bella? I think it suits being called that outside. Don't you think, baby?" He turned to Dahlia next.

"Yes," Dahlia replied. "But honey, please don't bother the girl either; Axton is enough, for that matter."

"It's okay," Ella said. "It is nice to see you."

"What do you want to drink?" I asked Ella while the waitress served my scotch.

"A water, thank you," she replied.

"Sarah, one water for... Bella." I ordered to the waitress.

Cheers followed, and the night started well. More people came, we had good chats. The girls seemingly clicked, but I was not pretty sure if that was a good thing.

After two cocktails, Dahlia's power rose, and she no longer could stay sitting in one place. She took Ella by hand, and both went to the dance floor. Not long after, the microphone was in her hands, and she turned the night into a concert of hers.

She was born for the stage and always stood well on the podium of my clubs.

But what stood even better right now was Ella in front, moving slowly to the music beat. She was not as confident as the many girls around, even a bit clumsy compared to them or to Kira, who was also there mastering every dance. But Kira was out of my sight, and all of the others around.

The scotch tasted perfect in my mouth, as well as the smoke scent from my cigar, while my gaze enjoyed every single move of that little black dress on the background of the flashing lights.

My pulse quickened as the music slowed down, and my lust was no longer under control.

I walked through the crowd and stood closely behind Ella. While I pulled from the cigar, I placed my other hand over her belly. She turned her head back, probably ready to scream, but once she saw me, she managed to keep her calm. Her gaze returned to the podium direction, and to a quite unexpected surprise, her body responded to my vibe.

Her moves grew sexier, pretty seductive as I was pleasured by the light touch of her ass over my hardness underneath my jeans. I slid my hand down her thigh, letting my fingers press hard into her skin as they moved up again and grabbed the hem of her dress. She kept her dance under the same rhythm, moving her own hands slowly over her body until she reached her hair and weaved her fingers through it.

I traced the same path, reaching her neck. I squeezed it slightly, causing her head to rest on my chest.

"Keep doing that, love," I whispered in her ear. "I like to see you hot."

As I pulled from the cigar again, enjoying the pleasure, I felt the phone in my pocket vibrating. I took it out to check the message.

Run! was only written in it, sent by Sebastian Moore.

I sharply turned back. "Cade!" I shouted with full force. Dahlia stopped singing, and the music instantly paused. "Get the girls out here! Everyone out through the side exits!"

I gestured with my hands pointing in the direction while Cade ran toward us. Dahlia jumped down, and Cade took both her and Ella by the hands and rushed to the VIP exit with them.

Panic aroused, people bumped into each other.

"Hurry up!" I screamed as I was already surrounded by numerous security guards.

"We've got you covered, Boss. We'll get you out of here."

"Get the people out fir—"

In an instant, dozens of shots from machine guns broke through the club's panoramic windows. Glass flew in all directions. People lay on the ground; others fell wounded or probably dead.

I started to the exit, moving behind the live shield. Bullets kept flying all around.

Suddenly, the security fell down, and a searing pain shot through my stomach before my eyes shut closed.

Chapter 9.1 (Ella)

Ella□

It felt good to walk out. As good as something in my life could be. But there I was, walking into a nightclub, living a life, no matter what kind. I was desperate for the possibility to forget about Grayson and my past.

The heavy air that wafted through the venue corresponded with the flashing lights against the darkness, exposing, only from time to time, those who were settled comfortably in the booth area. Long-legged waitresses, wearing tiny pieces of fabric that I could hardly call skirts because the skirts in my mind should cover the ass, were giving away on their duty. As the judgment went through my head, I grabbed the edges of my dress, trying to pull it down as much as I could.

Our way stopped before one of the booths, and Axton and I settled down. While creepy feelings conquered me once I saw Cade, Dahlia's welcoming smile made me feel... great! I might not be in the best environment, but hell, it was the best I have had. So, I tried not to think about the basement or Cade's hammer overall, instead, I decided to adjust somehow and enjoy the night—a night when I was more myself while pretending to be someone else than in my life before when no one ever allowed me to express my feelings and thoughts.

Although I couldn't exactly tell Dahlia that I dreamt of living in a world where Grayson and such people, and even Axton and Cade, did not exist, I told her about my fantasy of being free and in peace. To meet someone who would love and care about me, someone who would caress me with tenderness and warmth.

She understood me, I could see it in her eyes. She has expressed exactly that with her music many, many times. That's why I loved her art—the lyrics of her songs often merged with my heart.

Along with her ability to listen and support, Dahlia had the gift to lighten up everyone's mood. She took me by the hand and led me to the dance floor—a place so foreign but exciting at the same time. My feet started moving by themselves, followed by my hips, my shoulders, and hands. When I was a little girl, I danced alone in the darkness, dreaming of being a princess in one of the fairy tales' ballrooms. But I didn't want to return to those times; maybe not a princess, but now I owned the dance floor. Well, for sure, it didn't seem like that from the side, but I felt it that way in my heart.

Everything got even better when Dahlia jumped on the podium, and her voice filled the space; flashing lights accompanied her beat and pace.

It felt so refreshing. I sang with her in full voice, not bothered about the people around.

But then, sudden shivers went through my body—there was someone behind. I turned my head to see Axton there, exhaling the smoke of his cigar. For a mere second, I allowed my eyes to travel over his chest, where the upper buttons of his white shirt stood undone—something I tried to avoid the whole night. Then the memory of him putting his shirt over his naked skin earlier in the house brought back that damn stupid desire that used to arise so very often, no matter how hard I wanted to deny it. Once again, my subconscious mind betrayed all reasonable thoughts.

I tried not to react, or at least to hide the way I did, and returned my gaze back up front.

Axton moved closer. Very close. His hand slid over my belly. I could feel his strong torso pressed to my back. I wasn't sure why he would do that; it wasn't like I was the most attractive girl around, but that was something I secretly wanted to feel, even though I wouldn't say it out loud.

Some sweet trembles went through my skin, sweet but also burning when his hand moved down over my thigh.

Being touched by a man has always brought only pain and disgust, as my experience was only with Grayson so far. But there was something so different now—Axton affected in an electrifying way.

The scent of his cologne and the light touch of his breath mixed with notes of scotch and cigar aroused senses I knew nothing about.

I let myself to surrender in what was the closest to an embrace and moved my hands up my body till I reached my hair and buried my fingers through it. The moves of my body came unexpected but natural somehow. The music beat, slow and tense, matched the mood, leading me all the way.

I felt sexy. Seductive. I grew provocative. The sensual way my bottom rubbed against Axton's body and the lustful way I felt him react—that was sexy for sure. It was hot. And I felt a thirst for more.

That was so not me. But I was someone else that night. And didn't care about that. While the raging desire grew hotter through my veins and the devil's hands burned over my hips, then up my chest to my neck, I couldn't care because, deep within, it was wrong. So wrong, and I knew that. But my body screamed how voluptuous it was.

"Keep doing that, love," Axton whispered in my ear, fully intoxicating my being, sending down my spine more shivers than I could handle anymore. "I like to see you hot."

The body language foreshadowed a different finish to the night, but Axton's sudden movement back and subsequent shouts put an end to that.

I didn't get what happened at first. But panic aroused, and the next thing I knew was that Cade had caught Dahlia and me by the hands and hurried to get us out of the club. The following horror caused by the incessant gunshots sent people running for their lives. For a difference, our lives were secured by the cover of the security guards and the VIP exit we were privileged to use.

Everything happened extremely fast; I could catch my breath only when we got into Cade's car. The engine roared, and we sped off.

"Axton is still there!" I breathed out. I hated that this was the only thought that ran through my head; no questions about what happened or who caused the attack.

We reached the turn for the next block, but Dahlia only looked back and forth while Cade was focused on driving fast. Neither of them uttered a word.

"We have to go back for Axton!" I screamed, but there was no response. "Cade, stop the car!"

I had no idea what possessed me next, but I opened the door and jumped out of the car. I rolled several times on the asphalt until I was relieved I was still whole.

The sound of vehicle brakes made me swallow the pain, and I ran toward the club without giving a chance for Dahlia and Cade to come back for me.

I headed directly to the back entrance once I was assured there were no more gunshots. The screams had also died down; only muffled sounds could be heard in the distance outside.

"Axton!" I cried out after I entered the club.

It didn't take me any time to look for him, as I found him fallen on the ground only a few steps before the exit door.

"Axton!" I repeated as I crouched next to him.

I couldn't stop myself from taking a moment to look around before fully focusing on him. The setting looked terrifying—like after a war— it was smoky, suffocating. Poisonous it was.